No Time for That Now

Written by Jeannine Heil

Illustrated by PE Smith

Le Petit Chien Publishing

Park City, Utah

Printed and bound in the United States of America.

Printed by Paragon Press, Salt Lake City, Utah.

Layout and typesetting by Design Type Service, Salt Lake City, Utah

ISBN 0-9717019-3-8

For Mimi who loves the written word.
For the love and support of amazing friends.
In Memory of Willis.

Jeannine

For all my dogs. You know
who you are.

Patricia

Therapy animal (ther'ə•pe an'əməl)

1. an animal that has been certified and trained
    to enhance the quality of life through
    the human-animal bond.

Mitchell loves reading with his dogs.

Try though they might, lively Toby and shy
little Lulu cannot keep their eyes
on the words or their minds on the story.

As Mitchell reads on. . .

Toby and Lulu daydream of cozy beds,
fancy dinner bowls, and playing
with their therapy dog friends.

A hot air balloon soaring by their window grabs their attention and off the bed they jump.

They remember it's the Fourth of July!

Mitchell drops the book and they're out the door.

No time for that now.

Rousing piano music drew them into the theater.

Inside they found Musical Millicent turning pages.

Millicent!

"Sorry boys, can't you see I'm working?" Millicent woofed in a whisper. The pianist played faster and the dancers kicked higher.

No time for that now.

Off they trundled in search
of kindly Murfee,
    often found working
    at Mrs. Osguthorpe's
    house on the hill.

Mrs. Osguthorpe happily
    wrapped and slapped the yarn
    around Murfee's paws.

Murfee struggled to keep his
    furry body still and steady.

The boys grumbled off in the direction of the hospital where they knew Major Mac and Morty would soon be off work.

They found Major Mac and Morty reading with the patients in the hospital.

The library beckoned
to them. Mitchell remembered
story times when he had been distracted by a
big jar of lollipops the librarian kept on the top
bookshelf. . . and lollipops he LOVED.

Toby and Lulu recalled the jar of bones on the same shelf kept for rewarding therapy dogs for assisting in the reading program. And dog bones they LOVED.

This was their **BIG** chance.

The silence of the empty band room was shattered by the blast of a horn.

Into the darkened library, the little group lumbered and bumped along behind the big bass drum.

Lulu balanced on top to avoid being squashed.

THE DOG BEACH DIET

THREE DOGS AND A PUPPY

DOG VINCI CODE

WHO MOVED MY POODLE

THE STEPFORD PUPPIES

THE DOGS OF WRATH

CANNERY GROWL

HUCKLEBERRY DOG

DOG FATHER TOO

101 SCHNOODLES

UP
UP
UP

UP
UP
UP

the lollipops
seemed to be at a
dizzying height.

The dog bones
definitely seemed
out of reach.

As the dogs held the drum. . .

Steady. . .

Steady. . .

Mitchell stumbled.

Toby bumbled.

Books tumbled from the shelves.

Lollipops were jumbled.
Dog bones crumbled.

Lulu cried.

Alarmed by the blast, Major Mac barked orders to abandon the parade and run toward the library.

Someone was in trouble.

Lulu passed the scarf to Major Mac and he snapped the dogs into a line. Working together they'd have the strength to pull the drum off Mitchell and Toby.

Grunting and straining, Major Mac heaved the creaky old window open.

Out of the darkness

three bodies took flight.

The next day when the gang invited them out to play, Toby and Lulu were busy studying with Mitchell.

Their close call had taught them the value of helping others and had warmed their hearts.

They had decided to become therapy dogs . . .

. . . they finally had time for that.

HOW TO BE A THERAPY ANIMAL